Praise for The Imagination Station® books

These books are a great combination of history and adventure in a clean manner perfect for young children.

—Margie B., *My Springfield Mommy* blog

These books will help my kids enjoy history.

—Beth S., third-grade public school teacher

Colorado Springs, Colorado

[The Imagination Station books] focus on God much more than the Magic Tree House books do.

—Emilee, age 7, Waynesboro, Pennsylvania

My nine-year-old son has already read [the first two books], one of them twice. He is very eager to read more in the series too. I am planning on reading them out loud to my younger son.

—Abbi C., mother of four, Minnesota

FOCUS ON THE FAMILY® PRESENTS

THE IMAGINATION STATION®

Attack at the Arena

BOOK 2

**MARIANNE HERING • PAUL McCUSKER
ILLUSTRATED BY DAVID HOHN**

TYNDALE

FOCUS ON THE FAMILY • ADVENTURES IN ODYSSEY
TYNDALE HOUSE PUBLISHERS, INC. • CAROL STREAM, ILLINOIS

Dedicated to Jim Ware, an inspiration

Library of Congress Cataloging-in-Publication Data

Hering, Marianne.
Attack in the arena / by Marianne Hering and Paul McCusker; illustrated by David Hohn.
    p. cm. -- (Imagination station book ; #2) "Focus on the Family."
 Summary: Patrick and his cousin Beth travel back in time to ancient Rome, where they meet Telemachus and help put an end to the spectacle of gladiators fighting to the death.
  ISBN 978-1-58997-628-3 (alk. paper)
  [1. Time travel--Fiction. 2. Cousins--Fiction. 3. Christan life--Fiction. 4. Rome--History--Empire, 284-476--Fiction.] I. McCusker, Paul, 1958- II. Hohn, David, 1974- ill. III. Title.
  PZ7.H431258At 2010

  [Fic]--dc22   2010034367

Printed in the United States of America
9 10 11 12 / 17 16 15

For manufacturing information regarding this product,
please call 1-800-323-9400.

Contents

Prologue

Mr. Whittaker is a kind but mysterious inventor. His workshop is in a large house called Whit's End.

Mr. Whittaker's favorite invention is the Imagination Station. The machine can take you anywhere you can imagine—it's kind of like a time machine.

One day Mr. Whittaker found a letter inside the Imagination Station.

The letter said this:

To save Albert, I need a Viking Sunstone before the new moon. Or Lord Darkthorn will lock him inside the tower.

Mr. Whittaker did some reading. He found out the Vikings had used Sunstones a thousand years ago. He tried to go back in time to find a Sunstone to save Albert. But the

Imagination Station wouldn't work for him.

What had gone wrong?

Next, cousins Beth and Patrick arrived at the workshop. The Imagination Station worked for them. So Mr. Whittaker sent them to a Viking village.

The cousins went to Greenland and had some adventures. They rode in a Viking ship. They saw

polar bears and reindeer.
They met Erik the Red
and Leif Eriksson. They
found a blue Sunstone
and came back home in
the Imagination Station.

The cousins returned to the workshop, and they found another letter. The second letter said that Albert needed a silver cup from Rome. The cousins rushed to get ready for their next adventure.

But they still had some questions:

Who was Lord Darkthorn?

Would they be able to help Albert before the new moon?

Most important—how would they find a silver cup?

The Second Trip

Patrick, Beth, and Mr. Whittaker were at Whit's End on Tuesday morning. They were in the workshop getting ready for the Roman adventure.

Beth came out of the girls' changing room. Patrick came out of the boys' changing room soon afterward.

The cousins were curious about their ancient Roman costumes.

"Why did you give me a plain dress?" Beth

asked Mr. Whittaker. "The cloth is rough. And the only thing pretty about it is the gold border." She looked down at the gray tunic. It reached to her ankles. The tunic was not long enough to cover her leather sandals.

"You need to blend in," Mr. Whittaker said.

"As what?" Beth asked.

"A slave," Mr. Whittaker said. "There were lots of slaves in ancient Rome."

"A slave!" Beth said. "No!"

"Don't complain," Patrick said. "I have to wear a bathrobe!"

Mr. Whittaker laughed. "It's not a bathrobe," he said. "The ancient Romans wore robes and tunics."

"But the belt is a rope," Patrick said. "And the hood is weird. When I put it on, I look creepy."

"No one in Rome will think you look creepy," Mr. Whittaker said. "In fact, that kind of robe was a sign of peace. It's what monks wore."

"Monks?" Beth asked.

"A monk is a holy man," Mr. Whittaker said. "They can live anywhere."

"I'm going to be a holy man?" Patrick asked. "But I can't even sit still in church!"

"It's better than being a slave," said Beth.

The cousins walked to the Imagination Station. It reminded Patrick of the front of a helicopter. He looked at Beth and smiled. She smiled back. The cousins wanted to get going.

They climbed inside the Imagination Station.

Patrick and Beth looked carefully at the dashboard. A red button was in the center. Around it were dials, levers, and flashing lights. On top of the dashboard were two letters.

Two very old and mysterious letters.

The Gifts

"Where is the blue Sunstone?" Beth asked Mr. Whittaker. "It's not inside the Imagination Station anymore."

"I put it on the dashboard last night," Mr. Whittaker said. "It was gone this morning. I think whoever wrote the letters took the Sunstone."

"But how could that happen?" Beth asked.

"I'm trying to figure that out," Mr. Whittaker said.

"I thought all the controls are here," Patrick said.

Mr. Whittaker frowned. "I built a remote control for the machine," he said. "I took it with me on my last adventure. I accidentally left it there."

"Can't you go back to get it?" Beth asked.

"I would if the Imagination Station would let me," Mr. Whittaker said. "It won't work for me right now. I'm trying to find out why."

"But who is Albert?" Patrick asked.

"Albert is an ancestor of mine from many, many years ago," he said.

"I want to write a family history," Mr. Whittaker said. "I took trips in the Imagination Station to meet my ancestors. I met Albert, and now he's in trouble."

"That's what the second letter says,"

Patrick said. "Albert needs more help."

Mr. Whittaker reached inside the Imagination Station. A fancy ring appeared on his finger. It was a square of gold with a rose engraved in the middle. The square had eight tiny pearls around the edge.

"Your ring keeps appearing and disappearing," Beth said.

"It was a gift from Albert," Mr. Whittaker said. "You can only see it when my hand is in the machine."

He picked up the letter and read:

More trouble for Albert. Lord Darkthorn is angry. The Roman monk's silver cup is missing. We need it before the new moon. May God be with you.

Mr. Whittaker put down the letter. He took his hand out of the Imagination Station. The fancy ring disappeared.

"Is there anything special about the silver cup we have to find?" Patrick asked. "There might be hundreds of them in Rome."

"It's a monk's cup," Mr. Whittaker said.

Patrick suddenly smiled. "That's why you have me dressed like this!" he said.

"A monk's cup?" Beth asked.

"A monk's cup looks like a goblet," Mr. Whittaker said. "Some people call it a *chalice*."

"What's so special about it?" Patrick asked.

Mr. Whittaker said, "A monk would use one in a holy ceremony called 'The Lord's Supper,' or 'Communion.'"

"Well, we won't find it sitting here," Beth said. She wiggled in her seat.

"You're right, Beth," Mr. Whittaker said. "But first I have something else for you."

He walked over to the computer desk and picked up two items. He brought them back to the Imagination Station.

Mr. Whittaker handed Patrick a wide metal armband. It had rubies in it.

"Wear that high on your arm." Mr. Whittaker said. "Keep it hidden under your robe."

"What's it for?" Patrick asked.

"A man will ask you for something of value." Mr. Whittaker said. "Use this."

Patrick nodded.

Mr. Whittaker gave a little leather pouch to Beth. "This is birdseed," he said.

"Birdseed?" Beth said. "Don't Roman birds get enough to eat?" She tucked the pouch into her belt.

"You'll understand when the time comes," Mr. Whittaker said. He gave Beth a knowing wink. Mr. Whittaker closed the Imagination Station's doors.

Beth pushed the red button.

The Imagination Station started to shake. Then it rumbled. It seemed to move.

Beth took a quick breath. She closed her eyes. The machine jerked forward.

Patrick felt as if he were on the subway. He pushed his body into the seat and waited.

The rumble grew louder.

The machine whirled.

Suddenly, everything went black.

The Growl

Patrick and Beth blinked. A bright light replaced the darkness of the Imagination Station. It was the sun. They felt a breeze move against their faces. Their feet settled on warm sand.

The Imagination Station slowly faded.

The cousins looked around. They were in a huge empty arena.

"It's as big as a pro baseball stadium," Patrick said.

"The walls are amazing," said Beth.

Rrrowl.

The sound came from behind them. The cousins spun around.

They were suddenly looking at a black-and-orange tiger. The two froze with fear. The tiger was only twenty yards away. It gazed at them and growled again.

"What do we do?" Beth asked. "Do we stand still or run away?"

The tiger took a step toward them.

"Run!" Patrick yelled.

The cousins turned and ran. The arena was a large oval of sand and tall walls. The many doorways were blocked by metal bars.

There was nowhere to hide.

The cousins zigged. They zagged. Their feet kicked up a spray of sand.

The tiger followed slowly. It seemed to know the kids were an easy lunch. It couldn't be bothered to hurry after them.

"This way!" a man's voice shouted. "Come to this door!"

The cousins turned and ran toward the voice. They could hear the tiger's paws thump on the sand. It was moving faster now.

The door was only a few steps away.

But so was the tiger.

Rrrowl!

The Boar

All of a sudden, there was a loud creak. The metal bars in the doorway moved upward. Sharp spikes were at the bottom of the bars.

Squeal!

An animal shot out of the opening like a bullet.

Beth gasped. "It's a boar!"

The tiger's attention moved from the cousins to the large wild pig.

The boar grunted. It trotted around and

sniffed the ground.

The tiger crouched as if it might pounce. Then the boar seemed to realize it was in danger. It squealed loudly and ran away.

The tiger sprang after the wild pig.

The boar squealed again. It ran in tight circles.

The tiger chased it.

Beth heard the creaking sound behind them again. The metal bars had lifted farther up.

Patrick heard the noise too, and he turned.

A man stood in the doorway behind the bars. He was holding a long whip. He wore a short-sleeved tunic just like Beth's. It even had a gold border. It was the clothing of a slave.

The man waved his hand for Patrick and Beth to come to him.

Beth got there first and rolled under the bars. She was careful to stay away from the spikes.

Next the man made a loud kissing sound with his lips. The boar seemed to hear the noise. It quickly changed direction. Then it ran straight under the bars.

Patrick followed. He slid under the bars as if he were sliding into home plate. Dust filled the air.

"No!" Beth screamed.

Patrick's belt was caught on a spike. He was trapped. The top half of his body was still inside the arena.

Patrick hoped the tiger had given up. But no—the animal crouched down like a cat searching for a mouse. Its eyes burned bright. It ran straight toward Patrick.

Patrick couldn't look. He covered his head with his arms.

Whoosh!

Beth threw a handful of sand at the tiger's face. "Take that," she shouted.

The tiger slowed. It shook its head.

"Back!" the slave shouted. He quickly rolled into the arena and jumped to his feet. He brought out a whip and snapped it.

Crack!

The whip cracked the air. The tiger flinched and stopped.

Another *crack*!

The tiger backed up, snarling.

The slave cracked the whip again.

This time the tiger swatted at the whip.

Rrrowl.

Crack!

The tiger flattened its ears and hissed. It swiped a paw at the whip.

Rrrowl.

Crack!

Beth tugged on Patrick's belt. The rope came loose.

Patrick twisted and turned to wriggle himself through the opening. Finally he passed under the bars.

"He's safe," Beth called to the slave.

The man flicked the whip one last time. Then he crawled under the bars. He flipped a lever on the wall. The metal spikes crashed down into the dirt.

The tiger gave one last growl and trotted off.

Patrick, Beth, and the slave moved into a

dark, narrow hallway. They leaned against a cool stone wall.

"Phew," Patrick said, "that was close." He wiped a bead of sweat from his forehead.

"Thank you," Beth said to the man.

"What are you doing here?" the slave asked. "Did the emperor send you? Are you here to report on the animals?"

He rubbed a hand through his thick, curly black hair. One of his front teeth was missing.

"We got lost," Patrick said.

The man looked at Patrick's brown outfit and frowned. "You must be *very* lost if you're a monk in the arena. You shouldn't be here. You could have ruined everything."

"Yeah," Patrick said, puzzled. "Getting eaten by a tiger would have wrecked my day."

The man snorted. "I don't care about *your* day," he said. "The tiger must be hungry for the games tomorrow. If it had eaten you, I would be in big trouble."

Patrick looked surprised. "You weren't saving us?" he asked.

The man shook his head. "I was saving myself from a whipping," he said. "The tiger must be hungry so it'll fight harder. The harder it fights, the better the show."

"Show?" Patrick asked.

"The fight-to-the-death games," the man said. "You must have come from far away not to know about the games."

"Farther than you know," Patrick said.

"Thank you for helping us anyway," Beth said.

"Now I have work to do," the man said. "If

I were you, I'd get out of here. This place will soon be filled with soldiers and prisoners."

He jabbed a finger at Beth. "They may put *you* to work," he said.

The slave eyed Patrick next. "And *you* might be used for target practice," he said.

"How can we get out of here?" Beth asked.

The man waved his arm. "Go down that hallway," he said. "Turn left and follow the sunlight. You'll come to a doorway leading out of the arena."

"Where should we go once we're outside?" Beth asked.

"How am I supposed to know? Go back to your master," the slave said. "Or go to church and pray."

"Where is the nearest church?" Patrick asked.

The man burst into laughter. "That's very funny," he said. "A monk asking *me* where a church is!"

The slave turned away from Beth and Patrick. "You're on your own now," he said. He laughed again as he walked down the hallway. The sound echoed off the stone walls.

The City Gate

The cousins walked down the narrow hallway and turned left. They found themselves in a wider hallway. Sunlight streamed in from somewhere just ahead.

The hallway floors were stone. All the doorways were arched. Beautiful white marble columns held up the plastered ceilings. Colorful pictures of animals, people, and sea battles were painted on the walls.

Beth touched one of the paintings.

She felt tiny bumps of plaster under her fingertips. "My art teacher told me about those kinds of paintings," Beth said. "They're called *frescoes*."

The cousins heard footsteps echo down the hallway. Lots of footsteps.

"It might be soldiers," Patrick said. "Let's get out of here. I don't want them to use me for target practice."

They looked around. Where should they go?

Beth pointed to a staircase. "Let's go up," she said. "We can look out over the city. Maybe we'll see a church."

Beth and Patrick ran up three flights of stairs. At the top, there were more hallways and more stairs.

"This place is a maze," Patrick said. He leaned against a wall to catch his breath.

Beth's gaze went to marble statues lining the hallways. "Wow! It's like an art museum!" she said.

Beth went to one of the marble figures standing in an arched window. She looked out of the window. She had a clear view of the city with its crowded rooftops, towers, and tall trees. A wall circled everything like a fortress. Her eyes went down to a large gate in the wall.

Beth gasped. "Patrick, look at this!" she called.

Patrick joined her. "Soldiers," he said. Hundreds of them were coming into the city.

The soldiers marched in like an army of ants on green hills. They flooded the stone streets and filled the steps of the white buildings.

The soldiers wore silver helmets with

crests of red feathers. Some had on red capes; others had on white tunics. They wore red tights with gold shin guards. Most of them held spears.

Along with the soldiers were people with their heads held low. Their hands and feet were in chains.

"What's going on?" Beth asked.

"It looks like a victory march," Patrick said. "The Romans must have won a battle. They're bringing home prisoners."

"But those aren't just men. They're women and children," Beth said.

"The winner takes everyone prisoner," Patrick said. He leaned forward and looked straight down. "More soldiers are coming through the gate."

Beth looked off toward the horizon.

"There's a big building with a dome on top. Maybe it's a church."

"It's worth checking out," said Patrick. "Let's go."

The cousins hurried down the hallway and found another flight of stairs. They carefully went down, being sure to walk quietly. They passed several floors. Finally they reached a doorway on the ground.

They made sure they wouldn't be noticed and then stepped into the courtyard. They hid near a bronze statue of a man with a crown. It stood about seven stories high.

"It's that way to the domed building," Patrick said. He pointed down a wide road. The street was crowded with people and food stalls.

"Let's mix into the crowd," Patrick said.

"That way we'll blend in."

The cousins passed buildings of wood and stone. The houses seemed piled onto one another.

The flow of people was like a strong river. The noise was like the ocean's roar. The smell was like wet gym socks.

More than once, Patrick had to move away from a loose dog. The cousins struggled to stay together.

After a few minutes, they passed a woman selling food. Her stand wasn't busy, and so Patrick asked for directions to the church.

"It's near the city gate—that direction," she said, pointing. "They call it the Bishop's Palace."

Patrick thanked her. The cousins were on their way.

"Follow me, Beth," he said. "I see the dome of the church." He used his elbows to clear a path through the crowd.

Beth followed. She didn't want to lose sight of Patrick. She kept her eyes on his blond hair and brown robe. She was so focused on Patrick that she didn't see the city gate ahead—or the soldiers who were coming through it.

But a soldier saw her.

He grabbed her arm suddenly and spun her around. They were face-to-face. His eyes were dark and angry. Around his frowning mouth were a short black beard and moustache.

"You, slave girl," the soldier said. "Who gave you permission to wander the city?"

Beth's mouth went dry. Her heart leaped

to her throat.

The soldier picked her up and threw her over his shoulder.

"Patrick," she called. "Help!"

The Monk

Patrick heard Beth cry out. He turned around quickly. She had been flung over a soldier's shoulder like a sack of potatoes.

"Stop!" Patrick shouted. He pushed through the crowd. He blocked the soldier's path. "Put her down! You can't take her!" Patrick said.

"I can do anything I want," the soldier said. He laughed, but it was not a happy sound. "I'm part of the emperor's bodyguard—and this is one of the emperor's slaves. Move aside, little boy."

Beth pounded on the soldier's back with her fists. "Let me go!" she cried.

"Ooh," the soldier said, "I feel a little flea hopping on my back. Is that the best you can do, slave girl?"

"She didn't do anything wrong," Patrick said.

"Nothing wrong?" said the soldier. "Why is the emperor's slave free in the city?"

"Why do you think she works for the emperor?" Patrick asked. He was hoping to think of a way to free his cousin.

The soldier looked surprised by the question. "Are you blind?" he asked. "Her tunic bears the emperor's mark: the bright gold border." He shook his head in disgust. "Enough with all this talk. I might get a reward for returning a runaway."

"I'm not a runaway!" Beth shouted.

Patrick stepped forward, but he was stopped by four soldiers.

The man carrying Beth turned on his heel and hurried away. Beth took one last look at Patrick. Her eyes were as shiny and round as the soldiers' shields.

Patrick leaped forward, but the men grabbed his arms. They roughly pulled him back.

"I wouldn't if I were you," said one of the soldiers. He pulled out a shiny sword. "Or you may meet the sharp end of my blade."

He pointed the sword at Patrick. Patrick struggled to step back, but the soldiers held him tightly.

"There you are!" a voice said. It was soft and low, and yet the voice still cut through the noise.

A man stepped into view. He had thick, dark hair and a long, dark beard. He was short and wore a brown robe. It had a rope belt, just like Patrick's.

"I've been looking for you," the monk said with a gentle smile.

The hands on Patrick's arms loosened.

One of the soldiers asked the man, "Does this boy belong to you?"

"To me?" the monk said. "All children belong to the one true God."

"Then take him outside the city," the soldier said. "Or he'll belong to the dirt when he falls from my sword."

The soldiers stepped back.

"Come along, then," the monk said gently to Patrick. He put a hand on the boy's shoulder. "Let's go now."

"I can't!" Patrick said. He pushed the monk's hand off him. "I'm not leaving without Beth!"

The monk leaned close to Patrick's ear. He whispered, "You have great courage, but you lack wisdom. Stay and they'll make you a slave. Come with me. God may let you find your friend later."

Patrick hung his head. The monk was right. There was no way he could help Beth. Not here. Not now.

Patrick gave the soldiers an angry glare. But he allowed the monk to lead him away.

"I am Brother Telemachus," said the monk when they were outside the city.

"I'm Patrick," he said. "Thank you for saving me from the soldiers."

Patrick followed the monk down a dirt road. He didn't say anything else, and so the monk said nothing more.

They walked for a long time. Then they came to a little hill. It was covered with trees. Spring snow covered the ground in the shady areas. Snow also dusted the leaves on each tree. Near the top of the hill was an opening. Patrick thought it might be a cave.

They climbed to the top of the hill.

"Welcome to my humble home," said the monk.

Home was a fire pit with some logs around it. Inside the cave was a pile of blankets.

Patrick sat on a log and buried his face in his hands. He was still sad and angry that the soldier had taken Beth away.

After several minutes, Patrick smelled

something burning. It was a strange smell.
He looked up.

The monk was cooking a lump of something
over the flames. It looked like it might be
rabbit—or what had once been a rabbit.

The monk poked the fire with a stick. "Are
you hungry?" he asked. "Come and share
my small meal."

Patrick walked over to the fire.

The monk took the rabbit from the fire
with the stick. He held it up and looked at
it. "This will do," he said.

Patrick wasn't so sure. He thought he saw
clumps of burned fur.

The monk took out a knife and began to
cut the meat. Telemachus offered some to
Patrick. Patrick politely said no.

The monk shrugged and sat down on

another long log. He bowed his head as if praying. Then he put bits of meat in his mouth.

"Do you live here?" Patrick asked.

"No. I live far away," the monk said.

"Why are you in Rome?" asked Patrick.

"God told me to come here," Telemachus said.

"Really?" Patrick said. He wasn't sure what the monk meant. "What does God want you to do in Rome?"

"I don't know," said the monk. He put another piece of meat in his mouth. "It is for God to know. It is for me to obey and go. Perhaps we'll find your friend."

"My cousin Beth," Patrick said. He was worried about Beth and where she might be.

Telemachus quickly lifted his head. The

monk seemed to be listening to something.

He nodded toward the trees.

"We're not alone," he whispered.

The Barbarian

Suddenly a man stepped out of the woods. He was large with wild brown hair. His beard was just as wild. He wore a leather vest over a long tunic.

Patrick braced himself. Was this man dangerous? Patrick got ready to run away.

Telemachus didn't look scared at all. He gazed up at the man. "Greetings, Brother," he said.

"I smelled the meat," the man said. "I

want some." His voice was low and raspy.

"You're welcome to it," Telemachus said. He handed him the knife and the rabbit.

The man took a bite of the meat. Patrick saw the man tuck the monk's knife into his belt. Patrick also noticed that the man's eyes darted back and forth. What was the man looking for?

The stranger asked the monk, "You're a man of God?"

"Humbly, I hope to be," Telemachus said. "You don't look Roman."

"I'm not," the man said. He spat out a piece of rabbit bone. "You would call me a barbarian—though I am a Christian."

"You have come far from home," Telemachus said.

"I was captured by Roman soldiers," the

man said. "They were taking me to the arena to fight. I'm not interested in dying, and so I escaped."

"I was at the arena this morning," Patrick said. "A man there said they kill animals at the games."

"Animals?" said the barbarian. He snorted. "You're worried about the animals?"

"Yes," Patrick said. "Aren't you?"

The barbarian scowled. "I'm more worried about how the animals will tear apart the prisoners. I'm worried the Romans will kill us all—just for sport."

Telemachus stroked his beard. "I knew such things happened long ago," he said. "But I didn't want to believe our emperor would allow it now."

The barbarian spat again. "Believe it," he

said. "The crowds will watch and wait for blood. Each time a man is hurt, the people will cheer."

Patrick heard shouts somewhere deep in the forest. The man heard them too. He threw down what was left of the meat.

"They're coming," the barbarian said.

"Hide in the cave," Telemachus said.

"No," the man said. "I don't expect a holy man to protect me." He pulled the knife out of his belt. He pointed it at Telemachus. "Do you have anything I can sell?"

"I have only a few worthless things," he said. "But they belong to God."

"Give them to me," the man said.

"But I am to take them to the bishop of Rome," Telemachus said.

"Give them to me now!" said the barbarian.

Patrick remembered the armband hidden under his robe. Was this the man Mr. Whittaker mentioned? Should he offer the armband to him? Maybe it would keep them from being harmed.

Before Patrick could speak, the monk said, "As you wish."

Telemachus looked behind the log. He picked up a small sack that had been hidden.

The barbarian moved quickly. He grabbed the sack from the monk. Everything inside it fell out. Something shiny clanged against the ground. It was a large silver cup.

Patrick's heart leaped as he remembered his mission. *It's the monk's cup!*

The barbarian picked up the cup. "You call this worthless?" he asked. "This chalice has great value."

"It was a gift," Telemachus said. "I plan to use it in Rome. I'll share the Lord's Supper with it."

"Not now, you won't," the man said. "I can sell this. I'll need money for my trip home."

There were more shouts in the forest. The sounds were coming closer.

The barbarian looked at Telemachus and then at Patrick. He held up the silver cup.

"I'm called Aldric," he said. "One day I will repay you for this."

Patrick watched as the barbarian ran off through the snow.

The monk's cup was gone.

Telemachus lowered his head. He looked as if he were praying.

"That was a bad thing for him to do," Patrick said.

Telemachus shook his head. "No," the monk said, "all that I have belongs to God, not to me. Let us pray the chalice will be used for good."

Patrick hoped so. He wasn't likely to bring it to Mr. Whittaker.

All of a sudden a small group of soldiers pushed through the trees. They used their spears to move the branches. The red crests on their helmets were dusted with snow.

"We're looking for a runaway slave. A barbarian," one of them said. "Have you seen him?"

Patrick looked at Telemachus to see what he would say. The monk said nothing.

A second soldier pointed to tracks in the snow. "There!" he said. "The barbarian went that way!"

The Roman soldiers ran off after Aldric. Their swords and shields clanked as they ran.

Telemachus picked up a dry branch. He threw it on the fire. The fire popped and sizzled.

"We'll sleep by the warm fire tonight," he said. "Then we'll look for your cousin in the morning."

Patrick wanted to protest. He wanted to find Beth right away. But he knew he should listen to the monk.

Besides, he didn't have a better idea.

Night fell and the moon appeared. It was a thin sliver. It made Patrick think of Albert and the mysterious letters.

Is the new moon here the same as it was in Greenland—is it the same where Albert lives? What exactly is Lord Darkthorn's tower? Could it be worse than knowing that Beth is in the hands of a Roman soldier?

The Emperor

While the monk saved Patrick, the soldier
had carried Beth away. He took her to a
large Roman palace.

Inside, they came to a large courtyard.
Beth could hear birds chirping and cooing.

The soldier dumped Beth onto the dusty
ground.

"You're not a very nice man," Beth said,
rubbing her back. She glared at the soldier.

He glared back. His eyes narrowed as she

stood up.

"What's that on your belt?" he asked. "A sack of coins?" The soldier grabbed the bag. The string didn't break, but a little of the birdseed spilled on the ground.

"What?" he said. "Only birdseed!" He let go of the sack and looked at Beth with curiosity.

"So, you're one of the slaves who takes care of the birds," he said and then laughed. "No wonder you ran away. I would hate to take care of the emperor's 'darlings.' "

Beth didn't understand him. She scowled and looked around.

Beautiful plants and small fountains made up a lovely garden. It was filled with birds: peacocks, chickens, and small brown sparrows. Noisy green parrots and white doves perched in the trees.

A stooped old man in a slave's tunic was leaning over a birdbath. He was pouring water into it from a bucket.

The soldier walked over to the slave.

"This slave girl belongs here!" the soldier said. "See that she doesn't run away again!"

The soldier turned back to Beth. "Do not leave this courtyard, or you'll be sorry," he said. He patted a bow that was hanging at the back of one shoulder. "I can knock a sparrow off a tree branch at twenty paces."

"Not in front of the emperor you can't," the old man said, mumbling. "You know how he feels about birds."

"Well," the soldier said, "the emperor's not here. I'm going to tell him I've found his slave. Then he may give me a reward—a large reward."

The soldier hurried off.

The old man said, "Now I can go back to counting the feathers in the emperor's pillow."

He walked away slowly. He turned to look over his shoulder. "Watch out for the peacocks," he said to Beth. "They bite."

Beth gave the man a small wave good-bye. She looked at the ground. A red chicken ran past her feet.

"I'm not a slave," she told the chicken. "I just look like one."

It cocked an eye at her as if to say, "And I'm not a chicken. I just look like one." Then it ran away.

At the far end of the courtyard, a gate opened. A young man came through. Beth thought he looked like a teenager. He began to make clucking noises. He rubbed his fingers as if calling the birds.

He walked over to her. "I've never seen you before," he said. "The soldier said you were a bird slave. Are you here to feed them?"

The young man came closer. He wore a tunic. It looked as if it was made of soft white bedsheets. It had a purple stripe down the front.

"Answer me, slave," he said.

Beth almost said no. But then she remembered the birdseed. She touched the pouch hanging on her belt.

"I have food for the birds," she said.

"Then what are you waiting for?" he asked. He sounded annoyed.

Beth opened the pouch. She began

to throw the seed to the chickens. The chickens clucked around her.

"They like your seeds," the young man said. "Do you have a name, slave?"

"Beth," she said.

"A common name," he said.

Beth frowned. "Oh really?" she said. "And what is *your* name?"

"Honorius," he said.

Beth put a hand over her mouth. She had to keep from giggling.

"That's a funny name," she said.

The young man turned bright red. He said, "You dare to laugh at your emperor?"

"Emperor!" Beth said. "You can't be the emperor."

There was a loud bang, and both of them turned toward the sound.

A

large iron

door in one of the

stone walls opened. A large Roman soldier

came through it.

"Your Highness!" the man said. He had

a deep booming voice. He pounded a fist

against his chest. Then, as the soldier came

closer, he bowed. "I am at your service."

"Greetings, General," said Honorius. "I

am glad you are here. Please

put this girl in prison."

The general looked at Beth and then back at Honorius. The general's bushy eyebrows lifted high.

"What did you say, Your Highness?" the general asked.

"I'm sorry," Beth said quickly. "I didn't know you were a 'Highness.' I mean, you're young."

"Do you hear that, General?" the emperor said. "Punish her."

The general ignored Honorius. He said, "Forgive me, O Great One. But you sent for me. I am to give you my report."

"I did? You are?" Honorius asked.

"Yes," the general said. "I am here to report that your army has won. The soldiers captured the barbarians. The prisoners are now in Rome."

"Wonderful!" the young emperor said. Then he frowned. "And why is this important to me?"

"The games begin tomorrow," the general said. "We will enjoy watching our enemies suffer and die."

"Oh yes!" Honorius said. "But I won't go without my birds. The birds must come with me."

The general bowed and said, "Whatever you desire, Most High One." He turned and walked away.

"Most High One?" Beth asked.

Honorius raised an eyebrow. "It is good that my birds like your seeds," he said. "Or I would chain you up myself. You are a rude little girl. But today I will spare you."

"Thank you, Your Emperor-ness,"

Beth said. And she silently thanked Mr. Whittaker for giving her the birdseed.

"Now," Honorius said, "we must begin to gather the birds."

"We do?" she asked. "Why?"

"You heard the general! We go to the games," he said. "We can't leave my darlings alone. You must collect them."

"You're taking me to the games?" she asked.

"I'm taking the *birds* to the games," he said. "You're coming to take care of them."

Beth frowned and said, "But the general just said that people are going to die there."

"Of course they will," he said. He gave a snort. "What's the point of a fight to the death if no one dies? Now get to work. It will take you most of the night to gather my birds."

Beth gulped. "Most of the *night*?" she asked.

"At the very least," the emperor said.

The Armband

The next morning Patrick walked with
Telemachus to Rome. More visitors were
coming into the city. The road was dusty.
It was filled with people walking or riding
on horses or donkeys. Some people were in
wagons pulled by mules or goats.

Patrick and the monk waited for their
turn to enter the gate.

"Where should we look for my cousin
Beth?" Patrick asked.

"The arena," said Telemachus.

"Why would the soldier take her there?" Patrick asked.

The monk closed his eyes and smiled. "I don't know," he said.

Patrick said, "Then why—"

"Because God has told me to go there," Telemachus said.

"He *told* you?" Patrick asked.

Telemachus nodded. "In my prayers this morning," he said.

"But what if she isn't there?" Patrick asked.

Telemachus stopped in his tracks. He turned to Patrick. "My son, there is no *what if?* with God. When He speaks, we're to listen and obey."

When they got to the arena, the entrances

were crowded. It was like a round hive with bees crawling in from all sides. It seemed as if everyone in the entire world wanted inside.

Telemachus and Patrick waited in a long line.

A man with a long robe and a scraggly beard was shouting nearby. "Tickets! The best in the arena," he called. "Get your tickets here."

Patrick tugged on Telemachus's sleeve. "Maybe we should get our tickets from him," Patrick said.

The ticket man heard him and came over. "Do you want to buy two tickets?" he asked. "I've got a few good ones left."

Telemachus waved him away. "No," the monk said. "We have no coins. We must sit in the free section."

"That's too bad," the man said. "The free seats are crowded and hot." He leaned in close to them. "Are you sure you have nothing of value?"

Value.

Patrick remembered what Mr. Whittaker had said. "I have something!" Patrick said. He lifted the sleeve of his robe. He slid the armband off.

Patrick held up the armband for the man to inspect. The rubies glinted in the sunlight. It looked valuable indeed.

"That will do," the man said. His eyes widened with greed. "I can get

71

you the very best seats with this. They are next to the emperor's box."

Patrick gave him the armband.

Telemachus reached out. "No, you mustn't," he said.

"It's all right," Patrick said. "Mr. Whittaker told me this would happen."

Telemachus gave Patrick a curious glance. But the monk said nothing.

The man handed Patrick and Telemachus a small coin each.

"Here are your tokens," the man said. "You may enter the stadium now. Just give the tokens to the guard next to the emperor's box."

"Thank you!" Patrick said. Now he would have a better chance of finding Beth.

Patrick and Telemachus stepped out of

line. They walked into the stadium and down the hallways. People sitting at tables sold all kinds of things. There were drinks, food, and jewelry. There were seat cushions and blankets.

This is like a baseball game at home, Patrick thought.

Telemachus was wide-eyed.

One table was set up with weapons. It had wooden swords and shields for children. Patrick slowed down to look at them.

Telemachus pointed to a spear tip and an ax head. "What are these?" he asked the woman behind the table.

"These are from past games," she said. "There are many collectors."

Suddenly trumpets blew loudly.

"Ah!" the woman exclaimed. "The emperor

is coming! Honorius himself!"

Patrick and Telemachus followed the crowd. Patrick had a sudden thought. *Maybe Beth is with the emperor!*

Patrick spun on his heel to go.

"Wait!" Telemachus called out. He grabbed Patrick's hand. "We must stay together."

Patrick and Telemachus followed the crowd into an upper hallway with arched windows. They found a space with a view looking down onto the city street.

More trumpets sounded. The gathering crowd cheered.

A parade with two rows of soldiers marched down the street. The parade moved toward a large entryway. The soldiers' shields and upraised swords shone in the sun. Then came large flags and banners. Next came a group of soldiers carrying a large throne. It had poles for handles.

The emperor was a young man with dark, curly hair. His robe was bright purple with a gold pattern woven in. He had a thin gold crown on his head. He waved to the crowd. They cheered for him.

"Honorius," Telemachus said to Patrick.

"He's so young," Patrick said. I

thought emperors were old."

Telemachus gave a little laugh.

The emperor raised his hand again. This time he held up a silver chalice. "To the good people of Rome!" he shouted.

Telemachus gasped. "That's my chalice!" he said.

"What?" Patrick asked.

"The chalice the barbarian took from me," the monk said. "How did the emperor get it?"

Patrick barely heard the question. His gaze was drawn to an object near the end of the parade. It was a large metal cage. It took six soldiers to lift it.

Inside the cage, birds flew around wildly. At the bottom, hanging onto the bars, was a slave girl.

"Beth!" Patrick shouted.

The Cart

Patrick raced for the staircase. He wanted to get closer to the parade—and to Beth.

"Stop!" Telemachus shouted.

Patrick ran down the stairs. He made it to the street level. Then he rushed out of the closest doorway.

The giant birdcage was still moving. The parade had turned. It was heading through a fancy entryway.

Patrick pushed through the crowd.

He moved closer to the cage. "Beth!" he shouted.

Beth looked at him. Her face lit up with joy.

"Patrick!" she cried out. She jumped to her feet. But the cage jerked, and she fell.

"Are you okay?" Patrick called. He jogged alongside the parade. He had to keep up with her.

"I'm fine," she called back. "I'm taking care of the emperor's birds."

Patrick was relieved. She didn't seem to be in danger.

The parade stopped inside the arena. The emperor waved to the cheering crowd.

Patrick moved in close to the cage.

"Have you found a monk?" Beth asked him.

"He's behind me," Patrick said. He turned to point out Telemachus. But the monk wasn't there.

"Uh-oh," Patrick said, "I lost him."

Suddenly strong hands grabbed Patrick.

"Get back!" a soldier shouted. He lifted Patrick off the ground. Patrick saw the soldier's face.

It was the same soldier who had carried Beth away. The same beard and moustache. The same dark, angry eyes.

"You!" the soldier said. "Trying to help this slave escape again?"

"Escape?" Patrick said. "But I wasn't—"

"I warned you before," the soldier said. He dragged Patrick away from the birdcage.

"Let him go!" Beth shouted.

"I wasn't doing anything!" Patrick said.

The soldier took Patrick farther back in the parade. Then the soldier picked him up and threw him into a wood cart.

"See how you like life with the enemies of Rome!" the soldier said.

Patrick fell onto the bottom of the cart. His face was in the mud and straw. Voices grunted at him. Large feet kicked him out of the way.

"Stop it!" Patrick said. He tried to stand up. But the kicking feet and rocking cart knocked him down again.

"I wasn't doing anything wrong," Patrick cried. "Help!"

Large, thick fingers wrapped around his arm.

"Here, boy," a man said. "I'll help you." He pulled Patrick to his feet.

Patrick looked into the face of the man who spoke. It was the barbarian with the wild hair. It was the man who had taken the silver cup from Telemachus.

"Aldric!" Patrick said.

Aldric studied him. "Do I know you?" he said. Then he seemed to remember. "You were with that little monk."

"What are you doing here?" Patrick said. "We thought you had escaped."

"I thought so too," Aldric said. "But the soldiers found me again."

"Is that how the emperor got the cup?" Patrick asked.

Aldric scowled. "I wondered what they would do with it," he said.

Patrick looked around. The other people in the cart were dressed in rags. They looked sad and tired.

"What's happening?" Patrick asked Aldric. "Where are we going?"

"To please the crowds in the stadium,"

Aldric said.

Dozens of other carts followed. They were crowded with men headed for the games.

Patrick could still see Beth up ahead in the cage.

The emperor's parade moved through the large archway. Now it was in the arena.

The cart jerked and turned. It headed down a ramp away from the parade. Patrick could no longer see the arena—he was underneath it.

"Why are we going in here?" Patrick asked. He was afraid to lose Beth again.

"Stay close to me," Aldric said to Patrick.

"Yes, sir," Patrick said.

One by one the carts stopped.

"Get a move on," a guard shouted at the prisoners. "Climb out of the carts." He cracked a whip over their heads.

The prisoners hurried out of the carts. Patrick was pushed with the men down a long hallway. It was lined with cells on each side. Some held more men. Others had caged animals.

Patrick saw dogs that snapped wildly. Foam flicked from their mouths. Lions paced in their cages.

A pair of tigers stared at him. Had one of them chased him only yesterday? And the boar was there with its long tusks.

A monkey screeched and threw itself at the bars.

"It's like a zoo," Patrick said. "What are the animals all doing here?"

"The same as us," Aldric said. "We're here to die for the glory of Rome."

The Games Begin

The parade stopped at the emperor's special seating area. The soldiers lowered Honorius on his throne. He moved to a chair at the edge of the box. He waved to the arena crowd again.

Beth was still in the birdcage. Soldiers placed it just behind the emperor. She searched the crowd. Had Patrick gotten away from the soldier?

A guard unlocked the birdcage door.

Honorius came to the cage.

"Hello, my little pets," he said. The emperor pointed out his favorite birds. He said to Beth, "Make sure they are near me—and happy."

Some birds sat on perches. Others simply wandered around Honorius's throne. They pecked the seeds Beth had thrown onto the ground. A white dove landed on her shoulder. It cooed in her ear.

She scowled at it. She had spent all night catching the birds. Now she was sick of them.

Trumpets sounded again. The crowd took their seats. All eyes looked down toward the arena floor.

Acrobats emerged from several doorways. They danced and did backflips. They climbed on one another's shoulders. They balanced on thin poles with one hand.

Beth couldn't help but peek at the show. But she also scanned the crowds for Patrick.

Next, jugglers appeared. They tossed up large balls and even burning arrows. One seemed to spit fire from his mouth.

"More! More!" the people cheered.

The metal bars in front of the doors had lifted. Slaves drove in animals with whips. Some of the beasts were chained. The slaves poked and prodded the lions, tigers, elephants, and zebras. They roared and trumpeted.

An elephant reared back. Its front legs came down on two men. Beth feared the slaves were badly hurt or even dead.

"Bravo! That's more like it!" a man in the crowd shouted. The people stood up and cheered.

Beth hid her face.

"What is wrong with you, bird girl?" Honorius asked.

"I can't look," Beth said. Her hands were in front of her face.

"What?" he asked. "Don't you find this exciting?"

Beth peeked up just enough to see his face. "No, Your Highness," she said. "I think it's terrible."

He tipped his head as if her words surprised him. "But the people love the games," he said.

"They shouldn't," Beth said. "Not if people and animals get killed."

The crowd continued to shout and cheer. Beth turned away from the emperor. She moved to the wall behind the seating area.

"Beth!" a voice called to her.

She looked up. A man in a brown robe was peering over the wall.

The Monk's Message

"Are you a monk?" Beth asked the man.

"I am Telemachus," he said. "I saw you when the soldier picked you up. Will you deliver a message to the emperor?"

"Yes," she said.

"Ask him if he is a Christian," said the monk.

"Okay," she said. "And then what?"

Telemachus told her what to say.

Beth frowned. "He won't like it," she said.

"Perhaps not," said Telemachus. "If he wishes to talk to me, I'm here."

Beth took a deep breath. She walked over to the throne.

Honorius was still watching the games. He was safe in his high seat. Nets protected him from wild animals. He was smiling and drinking.

She glanced at the arena. Slaves fought the wild creatures. The men screamed and ran when the animals attacked.

Honorius held the silver cup in his hand.

"Your Highness?" Beth began.

"What is it?" he asked.

Beth asked him the monk's question.

Honorius gave her a puzzled look. "Am I a Christian?" he said. "Yes. Of course I am. By law the emperor must be a Christian."

"There is a monk who asked me to say this," Beth said. "How can a Christian emperor laugh when men die? How can he then drink from a holy cup? That silver chalice has been used for the Lord's Supper."

The emperor looked at the silver chalice in his hand. His eyes widened with alarm. He stood up. "Where is this monk?" he said. "I want to speak with him!"

Beth went back to the wall. She shouted, "The emperor wants you. And I think he's mad."

● ● ●

In a cell under the arena . . .

Patrick wondered what to do next.

From somewhere above the prisoners, trumpets sounded.

The guard gave the men a mean smile. He shouted at them: "It is time. March two by two up to the doors. A soldier will give you swords and shields."

The prisoners stood silent.

"Enter the arena when the doors open," the guard said. "Then salute Emperor Honorius. Next, fight. The last man standing will be today's hero."

"This boy does not belong here," Aldric said to the guard. "We men deserve to fight and die. But he is only a child."

The guard drew out a sword. "He is nothing to me," he said. "Now, shut your mouth and march!"

● ● ●

In the emperor's box . . .

Honorius's bodyguards brought

Telemachus to the emperor's box.

The monk bowed to the emperor.

"What does your message mean, little monk?" Honorius asked. He held up the silver goblet.

"Your Highness is drinking from a holy chalice," Telemachus said. "I, myself, brought it to Rome. You now use it to salute death."

Honorius's face turned a deep red. "The people asked for these games," he said. "Rome's army pushed back the barbarians. Now we celebrate a war victory." He frowned. "Why would I stop the games?"

"Because you say you follow Christ, the Bread of *life*," Telemachus said.

Suddenly the crowd roared. Beth, Telemachus, and Honorius turned. The prisoners marched to the center of the arena.

Beth saw her cousin and cried out, "Patrick!"

The Birds

Most of the prisoners carried swords and shields. Only Patrick carried a large knife and a helmet. He looked confused.

The prisoners saluted the emperor. "Hail, Emperor!" they shouted. "We who are about to die salute you!"

The crowd roared and clapped.

Honorius held up his hand. "Wait!" he said. But his voice was drowned out by the noise.

The men in the arena raised their swords.

He said to wait! Beth thought. Panic filled her heart. *Didn't they hear him?*

A trumpet sounded. The prisoners began to fight each other. Each man battled for his life. An old prisoner quickly knocked Patrick's knife out of his hand.

The emperor watched angrily. He called a soldier over. "I told them to wait!" Honorius shouted. "Why do they fight?"

"Highness, you raised your hand," the soldier said. "The prisoners thought you were asking them to begin!"

The emperor sank into his chair. He wiped his face. "How do I make them stop?" he asked.

● ● ●

In the arena . . .

Aldric grabbed Patrick and pulled him

close. A slave came forward with his sword raised. The barbarian swung his sword to drive him back.

Patrick dropped his helmet. It was too heavy. He wanted to run. But where? Bars blocked all the doors. Men fought all around him. Two closed in on Aldric with their swords pointed at his heart.

● ● ●

In the emperor's box . . .

"Somebody do something!" Beth cried. "That's my cousin!"

The guards looked at one another. They waited for an order.

Honorius was on his feet again. He watched the action below. His eyes were filled with worry. What would he do?

Telemachus's eyes were closed as if he

were praying.

An idea flashed into Beth's mind. She hurried to the birdcage and opened the large door. She stepped in and shooed out all the birds.

They flocked into the seating area. The guests there shouted and moved away.

Then Beth took the sack of seed. She shook the seeds into the arena.

Seeds rained down near Patrick and Aldric.

The two dozen birds followed the seeds. They flapped to the ground. They flapped to the ground right in front of Patrick and Aldric.

● ● ●

In the arena . . .

The attackers were distracted by the birds for a few moments. Patrick didn't know what to do. He looked at Aldric.

Aldric looked up at the emperor's box. Then he smiled. He dropped his sword and picked up Patrick.

"It's your turn to fly, boy," Aldric said.

The Knight

The barbarian hurled Patrick upward with a mighty heave.

Patrick raised his arms. His fingers caught the beam holding the protective netting around the emperor's box. He hung for a moment, his legs dangling in the air.

The crowd went crazy. Some were shouting *Boo*. Others clapped. All eyes were on Patrick.

"He's escaping!" cried a man in the crowd.

A woman shouted, "He's going to attack the emperor."

Patrick swung his legs to the top of the netting. He climbed it like a ladder and crawled toward Beth.

Telemachus pulled Patrick into the emperor's box. The monk hugged the boy. There were tears in the monk's eyes.

Beth also hugged Patrick—and this one time he didn't protest. A small red chicken welcomed Patrick by pecking at his foot.

But not everyone was glad to see him safe. Two of the emperor's guards came toward Patrick. Their swords were drawn.

"Stop!" the emperor shouted. "The boy is with me!"

The guards stepped back.

The emperor looked as if he might say

something else. But suddenly a prisoner let out a heartbreaking cry. A man in the arena had been wounded.

The prisoners went still. And so did the people. The crowd gazed on the emperor for his decision.

Should the wounded man live—or die? A thumbs-up from the emperor meant the man would live. A thumbs-down meant he would die.

Telemachus turned to the emperor. He said, "May I?"

"You wish to decide the man's fate?" the emperor asked.

Telemachus nodded. "If it pleases you," he said.

Honorius motioned for Telemachus to step forward.

Telemachus moved to the edge of the emperor's box. He raised his hand—his thumb was up.

"In the name of Jesus who shed His blood for us," the monk shouted, "don't take pleasure in this bloodshed! Stop—in the name of Christ—*stop*!"

There was a pause. Everyone was silent. The prisoners in the arena were still.

Then men in the crowd began to shout, "Kill, kill, kill!"

Beth covered her ears as the voices grew louder.

Beth cried out, "No!"

Honorius came to the edge. He waved his arms at the crowd. "Stop!" he shouted. "No more killing!"

But the crowd ignored their emperor. They

kept shouting, "Kill, kill, kill!"

Honorius gave up. He slumped in his throne. The chalice fell over. Red liquid spilled on the ground. Then the cup rolled to the foot of a guard.

"Your Highness," the guard said. "Here is your goblet." He held it out to the emperor.

Honorius waved it away with a flick of his hand. "I never want to see it again," Honorius said. "Give it to the monk. I am not worthy."

The emperor looked at the crowd. His eyes were filled with sadness.

"So this is what we've become," Honorius said. "This is what I have allowed."

Telemachus took the cup. He looked at it sadly. "How can I offer this to the bishop?" he asked quietly. He looked at Patrick. "You take it. To remember what has happened here."

He placed the cup in Patrick's hands.

The crowd now screamed with fury. Red-faced men and women pressed toward the emperor's box. They shook their fists at Telemachus for interrupting the games.

"Stone the monk!" one man shouted.

"Throw him in with the prisoners!" another man screamed.

The emperor looked at Telemachus. "You must leave," he said. "They'll tear you to pieces."

"I'm not afraid of death," the monk said.

Honorius nodded to a guard, who stepped over to Telemachus.

Telemachus understood. He gave a small smile to the children. "God be with you," he said. "And may this day be the last of these terrible games."

The guard took him out through a small back door. Beth watched him disappear into the darkness beyond. "What about us?" she asked Patrick.

Just then a gentle breeze swept through the box. The Imagination Station appeared. The door opened with a *swoosh*. The roar of the crowd stopped all at once. Everyone and everything seemed to freeze in place.

"This is new," Patrick said. What was happening?

A tall knight stepped out of the Imagination Station. He was wearing full armor.

Patrick and Beth gasped.

"It's time that you left," the knight said. "The new moon comes quickly."

"Hey, you don't belong here," Patrick said. "Your armor is from England, not Rome."

"There will be time for talking later," the knight said. "Now hurry! You must tell Mr. Whittaker to search for the golden tablet of Kublai Khan. He'll understand."

The knight retreated into the machine.

Beth wondered about Albert as she climbed into the Imagination Station.

Patrick remembered the mysterious Lord Darkthorn's tower as the door closed.

Patrick looked behind him. "Where is the knight?" he asked. "Didn't he get in?"

"He disappeared," Beth said.

"But—how?" Patrick asked.

"Let's find out," Beth said. She pushed the red button.

The Next Adventure

The Imagination Station door opened, letting in light.

Mr. Whittaker leaned into view. "Welcome back," he said.

The two cousins gazed at him.

Mr. Whittaker raised an eyebrow. "Is everything all right?" he asked. "Did you find the cup?"

Patrick lifted the silver chalice. "Here it is," he said.

Mr. Whittaker took it. He looked it over and then put it on the dashboard of the machine. "Wonderful!" he said. "Thank you. But why are you both frowning?"

"We're confused about how it ended," Beth said.

"Come out, and we'll talk about it," Mr. Whittaker said.

Patrick and Beth climbed out of the machine.

Patrick spoke first. "What happened to Telemachus, Mr. Whittaker?" he asked.

"History is unclear about that," Mr. Whittaker said. "Some legends claim that he was killed in the arena. Others say the crowd stoned him to death. Still other legends say that the Romans listened to Telemachus. They had a change of heart and left the arena in silence."

"I like that one best," Beth said.

"So do I," Mr. Whittaker said. "We do know one thing for sure: Honorius stopped the Roman games because of Telemachus's courage. The fight you saw was the very last one."

"They said the last man standing would be the hero," Patrick said. "But it was Telemachus who was the hero."

"That's right," Mr. Whittaker said. "Or maybe you remember what Jesus said. 'Greater love has no one than this, that he lay down his life for his friends.'"

"Telemachus was ready to do that," Patrick said.

"But what about the knight?" Beth asked.

"What do you mean?" Mr. Whittaker asked.

"An English knight appeared with the Imagination Station," said Patrick.

Mr. Whittaker looked surprised. "An English knight appeared in Rome?"

"He said we have to find the golden tablet of . . ." Patrick frowned. "What was the name? Kabab Cubes?"

"*Kublai Khan*?" Mr. Whittaker asked with a laugh.

"That's the one!" Beth said.

Mr. Whittaker rubbed his chin. "The golden tablet, huh?" he asked.

"Who was the knight?" Beth asked. "Isn't it weird he'd show up without your knowing it?"

"It sure is," Mr. Whittaker said. "But he must be connected to Albert and our quest."

"He was in the Imagination Station. But he disappeared when we got in," Patrick said.

"How can he jump around in time?" Beth asked. "He helped us out when we were in Greenland."

Mr. Whittaker thought about it for a moment. "I have some ideas," he said. "But we'll talk about it later. Meanwhile, you should get some rest. You have a big day tomorrow."

"We do?" Beth asked.

"What are we going to do?" asked Patrick.

"You're going to China to find the golden tablet of Kublai Khan," Mr. Whittaker said.

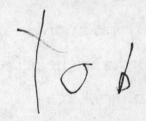

Secret Word Puzzle

Beth and Patrick searched for a silver cup. Now you can go on your own search. Find the *Attack at the Arena* words in the letter grid on the next page. (The words are hidden top-to-bottom or left-to-right.) Cross out the letters of those words. The leftover letters will spell the secret word—and you'll know where to find the special Bible verse on page 113.

Write the leftover letters, in order, on the spaces below. The answer is the secret word (Don't key in any numbers.)

___ ___ ___ ___ 15:13

1. arena
2. birds
3. chalice
4. emperor
5. monk
6. Rome
7. silver
8. slave
9. soldier
10. tiger
11. tunic

```
A S L A V E J S
R T U N I C M I
E B I R D S O L
N T I G E R N V
A C R O M E K E
C H A L I C E R
H S O L D I E R
E M P E R O R N
```

Go to **TheImaginationStation.com**
Click on "Secret Word."
Type in the answer,
and you'll receive a prize.

AUTHOR MARIANNE HERING is former editor of *Focus on the Family Clubhouse* ® magazine. She has written more than a dozen children's books. She likes to take walks in the rain with her golden retriever, Chase.

ILLUSTRATOR DAVID HOHN draws and paints books, posters, and projects of all kinds. He works from his studio in Portland, Oregon.

AUTHOR PAUL McCUSKER is a writer and director for *Adventures in Odyssey.*® He has written over fifty novels and dramas. Paul likes peanut butter-and-banana sandwiches and wears his belt backward.

FOCUS ON THE FAMILY®

No matter who you are, what you're going through, or what challenges your family may be facing, we're here to help. With practical resources —like our toll-free Family Help Line, counseling, and Web sites— we're committed to providing trustworthy, biblical guidance, and support.

Clubhouse Jr.

Creative stories, fascinating articles, puzzles, craft ideas, and more are packed into each issue of *Focus on the Family Clubhouse Jr.*® magazine. You'll love the way this bright and colorful magazine reinforces biblical values and helps boys and girls (ages 3–7) explore their world.
Subscribe now at Clubhousejr.com.

Clubhouse

Through an appealing combination of encouraging content and entertaining activities, *Focus on the Family Clubhouse*® magazine (ages 8–12) will help your children—or kids you care about—develop a strong Christian foundation. **Subscribe now at Clubhousemagazine.com.**